GORILLA WALK

*For Sebastian,
Happy Trails!*

GORILLA

LOTHROP, LEE & SHEPARD BOOKS ⋄ New York

WALK

TED & BETSY LEWIN

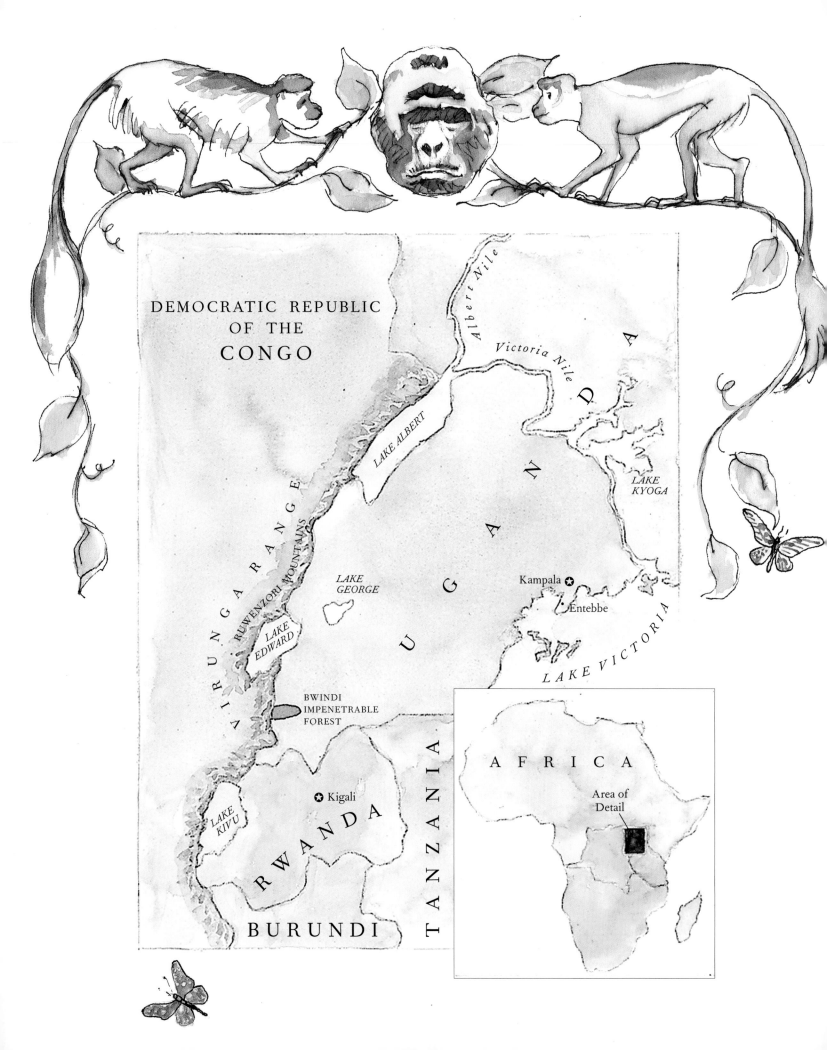

INTRODUCTION

In 1905, a German army officer named Oscar Von Beringe decided to climb Mount Sabinio in Africa's Virunga Range, hoping to impress the local chiefs and other colonial powers with German military might. While camped on a steep ridge, he encountered and shot two large manlike apes, one of which he brought back. Von Beringe's specimen was the first mountain gorilla ever seen by western scientists. Though mountain gorillas probably never existed in huge numbers, today only six hundred remain in the world.

There are three subspecies of gorillas—the eastern lowland, found in the rain forest of the Congo; the western lowland, found in western Africa; and the mountain gorilla, found only in the Virunga Range of Rwanda, the Congo, and Uganda, and in the tiny Impenetrable Forest in Uganda. Because mountain gorillas live at higher altitudes, they are the bulkiest and have the longest, thickest coats.

The relationship between mountain gorillas and humans has been tragic. Gorillas' heads are valued as trophies; their hands are made into ashtrays. Adult gorillas will fiercely defend their young, so the adults are often killed by poachers stealing the babies for illegal trade in endangered animals. Gorillas are maimed by poachers' snares intended for other forest creatures. And their habitat has been exploited for logging, mining, and agriculture.

In the twenty years after Von Beringe's discovery of the mountain gorilla, at least fifty were killed or captured in the Virungas. To protect them, in 1925 the Belgian colonial government of what is now Rwanda created Africa's first national park, the Albert National Park. By the 1950s, George Schaller, the first person to study mountain gorillas in the wild, estimated a population of four hundred fifty. By 1980, the population had dropped to two hundred fifty. The park had been split, the middle section given away, and almost half the gorilla habitat had been turned over to agriculture. Civil war and poaching also accounted for many deaths.

The mountain gorillas in Uganda have fared somewhat better. In 1932, the area of Bwindi was set aside as the Impenetrable Forest Reserve, which became Bwindi National Park in 1991 and is now called Bwindi Impenetrable National Park. The park lies entirely within the country of Uganda and is small and carefully managed.

Olive baboons

The black-fronted duiker is very shy.

In the local language, *Bwindi* means "a muddy, swampy place full of darkness." It is one of the few forests in the world to have survived the Pleistocene era, the time of the glaciers, and is well over twenty-five thousand years old. It is home to some species of animals, birds, butterflies, and trees that can be found nowhere else on earth. And today it is home to three hundred mountain gorillas, half the world's population. Of these, three groups totaling about thirty individuals have been habituated (made comfortable in the presence of humans) and can be visited by tourists.

Habituating mountain gorillas takes up to two years and is not an easy process for either the Ugandan trackers who do it or the gorillas. The trackers begin by following a specific group of wild gorillas daily. As they draw closer, the gorillas will either charge or run away at first, but gradually the trackers are able to shorten the distance between them and the gorillas. This takes both patience and courage, for even when faced with a charging gorilla, the trackers must remain calm, making the belching sounds of the gorillas to reassure them. The process must be very stressful for both gorillas and trackers at first, but over time the gorillas accept the presence of humans and behave quite normally.

Habituation is, however, not yet complete, for although the gorillas are now habituated to Africans, they are not yet habituated to white people. So white volunteers are recruited to accompany the African trackers, and the process begins again.

Black-and-white colobus

Red-tailed monkey

L'Hoest's monkey

Despite the difficulty of habituation, it has become critical to saving the mountain gorilla. Because of it, wild gorillas can be visited by tourists, which brings in a lot of foreign revenue, making the mountain gorilla both an important natural resource and a source of national pride. The first gorilla ecotourism, started in Rwanda in 1978, was a huge success both financially and for the gorillas, whose population has increased over time to three hundred twenty animals.

On the downside, habituation exposes the mountain gorilla to human diseases that could prove fatal. To reduce the risk of infection, visitors with permits are restricted to six per group and are allowed to spend only one hour with the gorillas. A minimum distance of fifteen feet must be maintained. Because gorillas have no immunity to childhood diseases, no one under the age of fifteen is allowed to visit, nor are tourists showing any sign of sickness.

Habituated gorillas are also much more vulnerable to poachers, who in 1995 killed seven. Four of them were speared to death while trying to protect an infant. The infant was taken and is presumed dead as well.

Interestingly, habituated gorillas are shunned by other gorillas. No one knows why, but in light of the risks of habituation, it makes sense.

Despite these problems, ecotourism seems the only way gorillas can be saved. As long as it generates revenue and jobs, it provides a strong incentive for the surrounding community to protect mountain gorillas and their habitat.

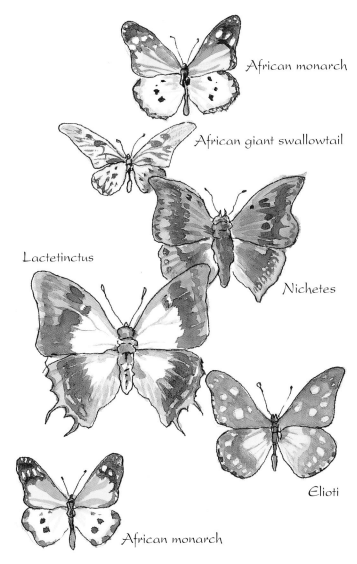

African monarch

African giant swallowtail

Lactetinctus

Nichetes

Elioti

African monarch

Emperor swallowtail

Nichetes

African giant swallowtail

When you're going to visit the mountain gorillas, Ugandans say, "Ah, you're going to see those people in the forest."

African Pearl Cottages

When we were kids, the only mountain gorillas we saw were pictures of dead ones, their huge arms tied spread-eagle between two trees, a pygmy posing dutifully beside them, spear in hand. Both of us dreamed of someday seeing these magnificent animals alive and free, but of course that wasn't even possible until the late 1970s, when the business of ecotourism began. Then civil wars and political chaos in the area forced us to postpone our journey several times. But finally, in November 1997, we are in southern Uganda, on our way to meet the mountain gorilla.

After landing at Entebbe Airport, we spent the night in Kampala. Now we're bumping along on a muddy rutted road in a Kombi. We've been traveling for nine hours and are still three hours from Bwindi Impenetrable National Park, with no sign of forest yet in sight—just endless terraced hillsides rolling back from the road.

As dark overtakes us, the green hills, now black, are shrouded with mist. The lights of a town in the valley below us look like fallen stars.

Endless terraced hillsides

Finally, ahead, we see the gate to the national park. Just beyond, lanterns have been set out like beacons on the front porches of the guest cottages, tiny, cell-like rooms with corrugated tin roofs. Once inside our cottage, we ready our cameras and gear for the morning, then flop into bed, exhausted. It's pitch-black except for the warm glow from the lantern on our porch.

The roads are really bad.

Our walking sticks

Ted with some porters

K GROUP

At first light, we step out onto the porch. Directly in front of us, the steep forested slopes of Bwindi rise into the morning mists.

By eight-thirty, we've picked up our gorilla permits (one hundred fifty dollars each per day). We're going to visit K Group, a small family of four: a silverback (only adult male gorillas have this distinctive marking), a juvenile, and a female with a two-week-old baby. We're told we'll be back by noon, so in addition to our rain gear, two cameras, twenty rolls of film, pocket tape recorders, journals, binoculars, sandwiches, hard-boiled eggs, and fruit, we've packed enough water for a three-to-four-hour trek—a liter apiece. We each select a stout walking stick from a bunch leaning against the wall of the park office *banda*, or hut, then pile into a small pickup truck. We'll start our tracking on the other side of the park, accompanied by two trackers, a ranger-guide, and one porter each to carry our gear.

Piling into the pickup

At the trailhead

A half hour later, we leave the truck, pass two guards armed with machine guns at the trailhead, and start down a muddy, well-traveled path, passing thatched-hut homesteads and neat fields of sorghum, potatoes, bananas, corn, elephant grass, and tea. A lone tea picker barely takes notice of us.

We climb up the terraced slopes. Behind us we look down on cultivated fields that stretch all the way to Lake Edward and the distant Ruwenzori Mountains. In front of us a wall of one-hundred-fifty-foot-high trees marks the beginning of the Impenetrable Forest.

Armed guards at the trailhead

The trackers hack their way into the dense gloom, and we begin to climb steep slopes, slipping on the muddy, rotting vegetation beneath our feet. Huge trees look strangled with vines. Giant tree ferns are everywhere, their trunks girdled with needle-sharp thorns. Long ropelike vines with thorns curved like cat claws snatch at our ankles. We stumble and grab for handholds but get handfuls of thorns instead. Our hands and arms begin to look as if we've been in a cat fight.

We set off.

We approach the Impenetrable Forest.

After climbing for two hours, we are soaked with sweat. So far, no gorillas. We slip and slide down sixty-degree slopes through moss-covered trees to an escarpment. Forty feet below, a jungle stream rushes along. K Group has somehow gotten down there and crossed to the other side, but it's too steep for us. We move along the edge, our glasses fogged, sweat pouring into our eyes and soaking our shirts. We pause to drink deeply from our water bottles. At this rate, we'll be out of water soon.

Covered with mud and slime, we slide on our backs down a very steep slope to the edge of the stream, then cross it on slippery moss-covered rocks, using our walking sticks for balance. On the opposite bank is a solid wall of vegetation and thorny tree ferns. The trackers hack and slice their way up the slope, lose the trail, backtrack to start up another way. We follow. Three difficult steps up, our boots barely gripping, we slide back down on our stomachs in the mud.

Betsy gets a couple of helping hands.

Black-and-white casqued hornbills

14

It's one o'clock, and the heat and humidity are dreadful. We drink the last of our water, then start up again, caked with mud, our hearts pounding from exertion, our faces sucked in from dehydration, our hair matted down with sweat. Ahead, the trackers hack away like machines, their green uniforms still smart and dry.

After five hours, we find gorilla tracks from yesterday—broken branches and fresh dung. The trackers whistle softly, almost inaudibly, to locate each other in the thick underbrush.

One step at a time, our walking sticks jabbing the mud, we head down yet another slippery slope to the bottom of a ravine. Here there is a stream so wide it creates a break in the forest canopy. Sunlight pours in, glistening on the coppery water that rushes over mossy rocks. We take off our steamed-up glasses, wipe the sweat from our faces, catch our breath, then cross the stream with helping hands from our porters.

Ted takes out a porter.

This would be easy if we were gorillas!

15

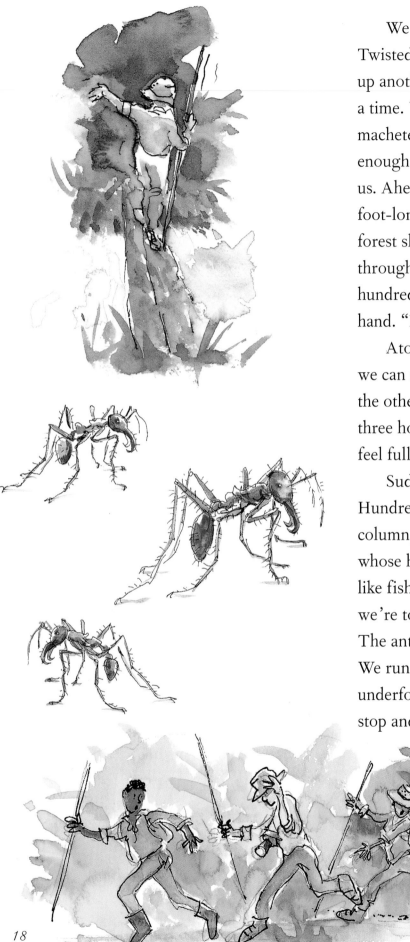

We come to a mucky ankle-deep swamp. Twisted roots grab at our feet as we cross it. Then up another steep slope, one step, one gasp for air at a time. We hear the slice and slash of the trackers' machetes ahead. They've hacked a tunnel just big enough to crawl through. Thorns and nettles tear at us. Ahead, a giant fallen fig tree makes a hundred-foot-long, rotting, moss-covered bridge up the forest slope. One false step and it's straight down through the thorns and rocks to the ravine hundreds of feet below. A porter offers a steadying hand. "Don't fall," he warns.

Atop the slope, the forest canopy opens up and we can see the sky again for a bit as we head down the other side. We've been out of water for nearly three hours now. We can't swallow, and our mouths feel full of cotton.

Suddenly our guide yells, "Safari ants! Run!" Hundreds of thousands of ants march in a narrow column, flanked by half-inch-long soldier ants whose huge mandibles curve backward at the tips like fishhooks. Their bite is like the sting of a wasp, we're told. "Hurry! Hurry! Run!" yells our guide. The ants seem to be the only thing he's afraid of. We run as fast as we can, crunching hundreds underfoot. When we're well past the colony, we stop and check our clothing for any hitchhikers.

We descend into a clearing fringed by tall trees and thick with brilliantasia, the dense, broadleaf bushes that are one of the gorillas' favorite foods. We've been tracking now for seven hours. We're soaked with sweat, smeared with mud, stained with moss, scratched and bleeding, unable to swallow in our thirst, out of breath, and without hope of ever seeing a mountain gorilla. The trackers, still fresh and clean, look at us and smile, then point with their machetes to a movement in the middle of the bushes. "There," one whispers. "The gorillas are just there."

They hack their way through the thicket to within fifteen feet of the silverback. Now we can smell his pungent, horsey scent and see the big black knob of his head. Slowly pulling back the tangled vegetation like a curtain, the trackers make "ahumm" sounds to reassure the silverback. And then, there he is, this gentle four-hundred-fifty-pound giant who moves through this thicket with such ease. Our thirst and fatigue are forgotten.

Rest stop

Red-cheeked cordon-bleu

Our trackers helped habituate this group and know them well. This one they have named Kacupira, which means "Lame One." His left hand is crippled from a fight with two other big males who ganged up on him in an attempt to take over his group. He was able to fight them off, but because he's handicapped now, the next time they may drive him away or even kill him. If they succeed, one of them will assume leadership, kill the baby, and start his own family. There can be only one leader, so the other male gorilla may stay with the group as a subdominant male, or leave to try to attract females and start his own group.

Our silverback is very delicately plucking the brilliantasia, peeling back the stems into curling tendrils and stuffing them and the leaves into his mouth. Our trackers make "ahumm" sounds.

Kacupira looks over his shoulder at us, passes gas, and continues to eat, then stops and seems to go into a reverie. "Ahumm." Kacupira rolls over onto his prodigious belly, rests his chin on the back of his folded hands, and stares directly at us from only ten feet away. He doesn't seem to really notice us, though; it's more as if he's staring right through us.

There is movement in the vegetation a few yards away. It's Kasigazi (Boy), the young male of K Group. Somewhere hidden nearby is Nyabutono (Small Lady) and her two-week-old baby, Magoba (The Prophet).

Before we know it, our hour is up. "Ahumm." Our trackers continue to talk to their old friend as we back away.

Yawning

Brilliantasia

We try to walk on the twisted root structure of the brilliantasia, but fall through up to our thighs. Thorns prick our legs, even through our pants. Hacking our way to the edge of the forest, we start back up the slope for home. We have to be out of the forest by six o'clock, and it is already five-fifteen. The sun will set soon.

After only an hour of hard climbing, we step out into a farmer's field. Had we known this morning where the gorillas would be found, we could have entered the forest from here and saved ourselves six hours of rugged tracking! Ankole cattle stand amid the banana trees and stare at us, their huge horns curving gracefully over their heads like misplaced elephant tusks. A long ridge flanked by terraced slopes descends into a valley. It's nearly dark now—six-thirty—and white plumes of smoke from cooking fires dot the landscape.

Banana tree

The road is still miles away as we start down the steep slant, bone weary, in darkness so total we can't see the porters in front of us and each footstep is an act of faith. As the slope becomes more gentle, shadowy figures pass us on their way home from the fields and the smell of wood smoke fills the air. An hour down, bottles of water are suddenly thrust at us out of the darkness. A ranger has come up from the road to meet us. We had almost forgotten our thirst, but we drain the bottles quickly. Still wet with sweat, we feel the chill of the night air.

Ahead now, we see pinpricks of light—the headlights of our truck. We walk into their glare and sink into our seats, exhausted. We've been tracking for almost eleven hours; we're worn out; we're shivering with cold; we've never been happier!

Golden-rumped tinker bird

Ankole cattle

M GROUP

A giant land snail
as big as a hand

At eight-thirty the next morning, we are walking down the rough road that bisects the park. Before long, we step onto a path cut into the thick vegetation at the side of the road and begin our climb. It's hard going, but after yesterday's long trek, we're ready for it. Today we're going to visit M Group, a group of sixteen family members.

After only three hours of chopping and slicing our way up the slope, we've found M Group's night nests: about a dozen flat, trampolinelike structures, bouncy underfoot. Forest foragers, mountain gorillas do not make permanent homes. Each gorilla makes its own nest every night, wherever the group happens to be at nightfall. Infants sleep with their mothers.

A night nest

We sit on the nests and look out at what the gorillas saw last night just before they dozed off. In front of us are three huge trees, arching at the top and hung with moss-covered vines. Through the graceful arch of the trees, the Impenetrable Forest rolls off, seemingly without end. We feel out of our own time; this view, it seems to us, is of the world first made.

A hundred yards up the slope we find M Group. Leaving our porters, we move quickly behind the trackers, come to a sunlit patch of brilliantasia, and stop, ankle-deep in a stream. The trackers wait, listen, then point directly ahead. Through the leafy cover, we see part of the huge back and shoulders of the silverback. He is eating. Then he turns to look at us, and all we can see are his eyes, hooded by his beetle brow. "Ahumm," say the trackers. We can hear the others feeding all around us, breaking stems and branches.

Butterflies on golden cat scat

Golden cat

The trackers pull back the vegetation. "Ahumm, ahumm . . ." Now in full view, the silverback—Ruhundeza (The One Who Sleeps a Lot)—is resting on one elbow. Kawere (Small Baby), a three-month-old, plays at his feet. Ruhundeza, the father of all the young in the group, is a tolerant papa. Kawere scampers up the great bulk of his father, then rolls off, head over heels. Ruhundeza lies back on the tangled vegetation and dozes, ignoring Kawere as the baby climbs on him again and again.

Kawere's mother, Bukuma (Lame Fingered), sits nearby, peeling the bark from a stem. She holds the peeled stem to her mouth as if playing a flute. Kawere, tiring of his game, joins her and watches, bright eyed. They both move nearer to Ruhundeza, feeding all the while.

Bukuma has a big round belly, as do they all. Gorillas' single-chambered digestive systems are not efficient for digesting vegetation, so they have to consume huge amounts daily (an adult male consumes more than forty pounds), spending about seven hours a day on concentrated feeding. This gives gorillas their bloated appearance. It also causes them to pass gas frequently. The rest of the day is spent moving, foraging, and resting. Gorillas sleep about nine hours a night.

Kawere stops feeding and crosses his arms. He looks like a little boy daydreaming. Bukuma begins to groom him. He holds very still, seeming to enjoy it immensely.

Ruhundeza sits up, halfheartedly eats a leaf or two, then lies down on his side. Bukuma goes to him and lies down facing him. Their faces only inches apart, they gaze into each other's eyes. It's such a tender, intimate moment, we turn our own eyes away. Kawere joins them and snuggles into his mother's back.

Ruhundeza's feet are pink and unblemished.

A juvenile, Bob, stands up and scampers sideways across the clearing, beating his chest with the cupped palms of his hands. He is showing off, imitating his father. But when a silverback beats his chest, it is a much more complicated, nine-step ritual that only an adult completes. He starts by hooting, then delicately places a leaf in his mouth, stands up, beats his chest, kicks out, runs sideways, tears up vegetation, then drops to all fours, and finally slaps the ground. Silverbacks do this to intimidate opponents and to assert authority.

Bob sits down about six feet away from us and stuffs leaves into his mouth. A female, partially hidden from us, sits up in a tree, breaking branches as if to build a nest. The rest of the group is spread out and can only be heard, snapping branches and loudly passing wind.

Our time is now up, and we begin to back away. As we do, Ruhundeza rolls up onto all fours and strides off into the dense thicket. Kawere pulls himself onto Bukuma's back, and she and the rest of the group all follow Ruhundeza.

Still standing in the stream, we are suddenly alone. In this dense patch of brilliantasia, surrounded by the Impenetrable Forest, in the heart of Africa, "those people in the forest" have left us behind.

MOUNTAIN GORILLA FACTS

"When the last individual of a race of living things breathes no more, another heaven and another earth must pass before such a one can be again."
—William Beebe
First curator of birds,
Bronx Zoo

Weight: Males 300–450 pounds   Females 150–250 pounds

Height: Males 55–73 inches   Females up to 60 inches

Diet: Leaves, fruits, shoots, stems, flowers, bark, grubs, insects (especially ants), ferns

Gestation period: 8.5 months

Estimated life span: Up to 50 years in the wild (There are no mountain gorillas in captivity.)

Predators: Man, leopard (There are no longer any leopards in Bwindi.)

Conservation status: Endangered

Gorillas are the most terrestrial of the great apes, spending over 90 percent of their time on the ground. They move quadrupedally (on all fours), walking on their knuckles, but can stand upright for short periods, particularly to reach food plants or as part of a chest-beating sequence.

LIFE CYCLE

Female gorillas reach sexual maturity at around the age of eight but usually don't have their first offspring until at least the age of ten. Gorilla pregnancies last for 8.5 months but are difficult to observe, since gorilla stomachs are always distended with food. Twins have been born to gorillas but are extremely rare.

Newborns have light brown skin and are highly dependent on their mothers. At first they cling to the

Knuckle walking

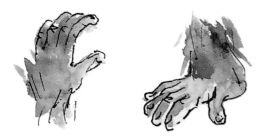

Hands and feet have opposable thumbs.

mother's chest, but slowly begin to spend more time on her back as they mature. During the second year, they become more independent and begin playing with others, interacting with the silverback, and feeding themselves.

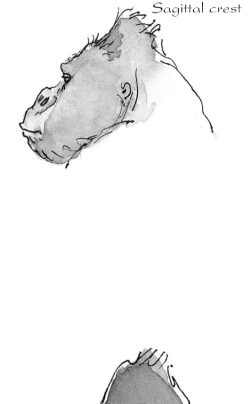

Sagittal crest

Classification	Approximate age in years	Description
Infant	0–3	A small animal carried by a female for long periods and weighing less than 60 pounds
Juvenile	3–6	A small animal not carried by a female and weighing 60–120 pounds
Subadult female	6–8	A female weighing 120–150 pounds, but not muscular, like a blackback male, and lacking a sagittal crest
Adult female	8+	A female that carries an infant for prolonged periods and weighs 150–250 pounds
Subadult male	6–8	A male weighing 120–150 pounds
Blackback	8–12	A male weighing 150–250 pounds, with few or no gray hairs on its back
Young silverback	12–15	A male weighing 250–300 pounds, muscular like an adult silverback and with a prominent sagittal crest, but smaller than a silverback. The hairs on the back begin to turn silver during this period.
Silverback	15+	A very large male gorilla weighing 300–450 pounds, with a prominent sagittal crest and a gray or silver back

COMMUNICATION

Gorillas communicate using a wide variety of vocalizations, gestures, and facial expressions. Sixteen distinct vocal signals have been identified. Adult males, particularly the lead silverback, dominate a group's vocalizations, and some calls are exclusively male and are often used in confrontations.

Nonvocal communications include bared teeth, a stiff-legged walk, lunges, and charges to signal various levels of aggression. These are often combined with vocal cues, as in the classic chest-beating sequence performed by adult males to intimidate opponents: The male hoots, symbolically feeds, stands up, beats his chest, kicks out, runs sideways, tears up vegetation, then drops to all fours, and finally slaps the ground.

Silver back

"At home, we talk of nothing but gorillas. As I fall asleep at night, I make gorilla vocalizations. And when I am asleep, I dream of gorillas."

—Richard Mageze
Ranger-guide
Bwindi Impenetrable National Park

INDEX

Illustrations are indicated by *italic*.

To Dr. George Schaller,
whose wonderful book first brought mountain gorillas into our lives

Special thanks to James Doherty, Curator of Mammals,
Wildlife Conservation Society

Watercolors were used for the full-color illustrations.
The text type is 15-point Fournier.

Published by Lothrop, Lee & Shepard Books
a division of William Morrow and Company, Inc.
1350 Avenue of the Americas, New York, NY 10019

Manufactured in China by South China Printing Company (1988) Ltd.

10 9 8 7 6 5
Library of Congress Cataloging-in-Publication Data
Lewin, Ted and Betsy.
Gorilla walk / Ted and Betsy Lewin.
p. cm.
Summary: Describes an expedition into the field in southern Uganda
to observe mountain gorillas in their native habitat.
ISBN 0-688-16509-5 (trade)-ISBN 0-688-16510-9 (library)
1. Gorilla-Juvenile literature. [1. Gorilla.] I. Lewin, Betsy. II. Title.
QL737.P96L49 1999 599.884-dc21 98-44727 CIP AC

At the time of this printing, K Group had crossed into Congo and has not been seen since.